Joanna

British Library Cataloguing in Publication Data

Kaye, Marilyn
  What a teddy bear needs.
  I. Title   II. Wheeler, Jody
  813.54 [J]

ISBN 0-7214-9612-1

dition

ed by Ladybird Books Ltd Loughborough Leicestershire UK
 Books Inc Auburn Maine 04210 USA
BIRD BOOKS LTD MCMXCI

gland (7)

What a Teddy Bear Needs

by Marilyn Kaye
illustrated by Jody Wheeler

Ladybird Books

In a toy shop, on a shelf, sat a row of brand-new teddy bears.
They all had fluffy brown fur. They all had big button noses.
They all had bright red ribbons round their necks. And they
were all smiling.

Except for Eddy Teddy. Eddy Teddy never smiled.

"You need to smile," the other bears told him. "If you don't smile, no one will ever want to take you home."

"I don't need to smile," Eddy said proudly. "I have the fluffiest fur and the biggest nose and the brightest ribbon. I'm the finest teddy bear in this shop."

Just then, a little boy and his mother came into the shop. All the teddy bears sat up straight and smiled their biggest smiles. All except Eddy Teddy. He just sat there.

"I want that one," the little boy told his mother. He pointed to the bear just to the left of Eddy.

What a silly boy, thought Eddy. *I've got fluffier fur than that bear.*

Then a little girl and her father came into the shop. "May I have that bear?" she asked her father. She pointed to the bear just to the right of Eddy.

What a foolish girl, thought Eddy. *That bear's nose is much smaller than mine.*

More and more boys and girls came into the shop. One by one, they each picked a teddy bear. But no one picked Eddy Teddy. Soon, he was all alone on the shelf.

I'm not going to sit here and wait any longer, Eddy decided.
I'll go out and find someone to take me home. He hopped
down from the shelf and left the shop.

Across the road, there was a big park where boys and girls were playing. Eddy saw one little boy playing with a very old teddy bear.

"Hello," he said, walking up to the boy. "My name is Eddy Teddy. And I will be your new teddy bear."

"No, thank you," the boy said. "I already have a teddy bear."

"But I'm a much better teddy bear!" Eddy said. "I have the fluffiest fur and the biggest nose and the brightest ribbon. I'm the finest teddy bear in the world!"

"But my teddy bear has something you don't have," the boy said. And he walked away, hugging his old teddy bear.

Then Eddy saw another little boy playing with a tatty old teddy bear. "Hello," he said. "Wouldn't you like a nice new teddy bear?"

"No, thank you," the boy said. "I'm happy with my own teddy bear."

"But your teddy bear doesn't have fluffy fur or a big button nose or a red ribbon," Eddy told him.

"I don't care," the boy said. "He's got something better."

Then Eddy saw a little girl playing all alone. She was the prettiest girl Eddy had ever seen. She had yellow curls and big blue eyes. He hurried over to her.

"Do you want a teddy bear?" he asked the little girl.

"Yes, I do," said the little girl.

"Well, here I am!" said Eddy.

"No, thank you," the little girl said. "You're not the right teddy bear for me."

"Why not?" asked Eddy. "I have the fluffiest fur and the biggest nose and the brightest ribbon."

"But you don't have what a teddy bear really needs," the little girl said sadly.

Eddy was puzzled. He was sure he had everything a teddy bear needed.

Then Eddy saw a rose bush. *That's what I need*, he decided. *A big red rose for my bright red ribbon*. He jumped into the bush to get the biggest rose.

"Ouch! Ouch! Help!" Thorns were pricking Eddy all over. He was stuck inside the bush and he couldn't get out.

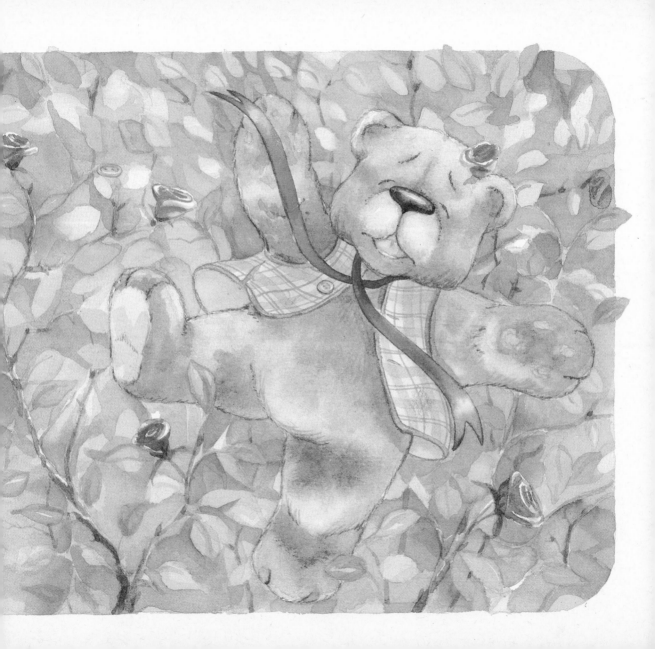

The little girl with the yellow curls grabbed Eddy's ears and pulled him free.

"Oh, dear," she said. "You've lost your button nose."

And that wasn't all. Stuck to the thorns were bits and pieces of Eddy's fur. And waving from a branch was his bright red ribbon.

"Oh, no!" Eddy cried. He turned away from the little girl and ran all the way back to the toy shop.

On the shelf sat a row of brand-new teddy bears. When they saw Eddy, they shook their heads. "You look terrible!" they said.

Eddy wanted to cry. Now no one would ever want to take him home.

Just then, the shop door opened. In walked the little girl with her mother.

All the teddy bears sat up straight and smiled. Except for Eddy Teddy. He hung his head in shame.

"Hello," said the little girl.

Eddy looked up. The little girl was standing right in front of him. She smiled.

And Eddy couldn't help himself. He smiled right back.

"That's the teddy bear I want," the little girl said.

Her mother was surprised. "But he doesn't have fluffy fur or a red ribbon or a button nose. Why do you want him?"

"Because he has the nicest smile," the little girl said.

The little girl took Eddy down from the shelf. Then Eddy knew what a teddy bear really needs. A teddy bear doesn't need the fluffiest fur or the biggest nose or the brightest ribbon. All a teddy bear needs is a great big smile.

And as the little girl hugged him tightly, Eddy Teddy knew that he would go on smiling for ever.